DEMETRI THE DRAGON
Learns to be Brave

written by
Julie Ivers

illustrated by
Diana Hernandez

This edition first published in 2024
by Lawley Publishing,
a division of Lawley Enterprises LLC

Text Copyright © 2024 Julie Ivers
Illustration Copyright © Diana Hernandez 2024
All Rights Reserved

Hardcover ISBN 978-1-960137-40-1
Paperback ISBN 978-1-960137-42-5
Library of Congress Control Number: 2023948846

Lawley Publishing
70 S. Val Vista Dr. #A3 #188
Gilbert, AZ 85296

LawleyPublishing.com

For Trey.—JI

**Demetri the Dragon was young but oh so tall,
And his dragon wings were weak and oh so small.**

He was scared to learn to fly because he might fall,
So until he could fly, he would walk, skip, jump, and crawl.

Demetri visited his mom later on in the day,
He told her his fears, and this is what she had to say:

"My dear, you're scared right now, and that's okay.

Give it a try—do it scared, that's what it means to be brave!"

So through the woods, he jumped and skipped a lot. Until he reached a nice grassy spot. Then he thought to himself, Maybe I'll give flying a shot."

"My fear of flying is as big as the sky,

But I can do it scared and give it a try. I'll do my best to

fly, fly, fly!"

FLAP, FLAP, FLAP, JUMP!
One, two, three!

Ouch!

Demetri lifted off the ground and hit a tree!

And when he tried to fly, instead he bonked his head.
He jumped out of the woods and back home he fled,
When he got there his mom smiled and kindly said:

"You were brave today! I am so proud.
Keep it up and soon you'll be flying in the clouds!

You might be scared and that's okay.

Give it a try—do it scared,
that's what it means to be brave!"

Demetri went to bed and woke up the next day. He walked, skipped, and **jumped** outside to **play**.

While watching the other dragons fly up and away.

He wanted to join them—
if he tried, he just may!

So through the woods Demetri marched with might.
He climbed up a mountain—no trees in sight!

Then he said to himself
as he prepared to take flight,

"My fear of flying is as big as the sky,

But I can do it scared and give it a try. I'll do my best to

fly, fly, fly!"

FLAP, FLAP, FLAP, JUMP!
One, two, three!

Ouch!

Demetri slipped and bonked his knee!

And when he tried to fly again, instead he took a fall.
Tumbled down the mountain like a bouncy dragon ball.

So back to his home
he would walk, skip, and jump,
until he could fly without taking a thump.

Demetri's head hung low, and he felt defeated.
Back home in his cave by his mom he was greeted.
And with a smile and open arms, she repeated:

"You were brave today! I am so proud.
Keep it up and soon you'll be flying in the clouds!

You might be scared and that's okay.

Give it a try—do it scared,
that's what it means to be brave!

Try again tomorrow, aim for the sky.
Flap your wings— one, two, three—
and believe you can fly!"

Mom always seemed to know just what to say.

Demetri would try tomorrow . . . tomorrow could be the day.

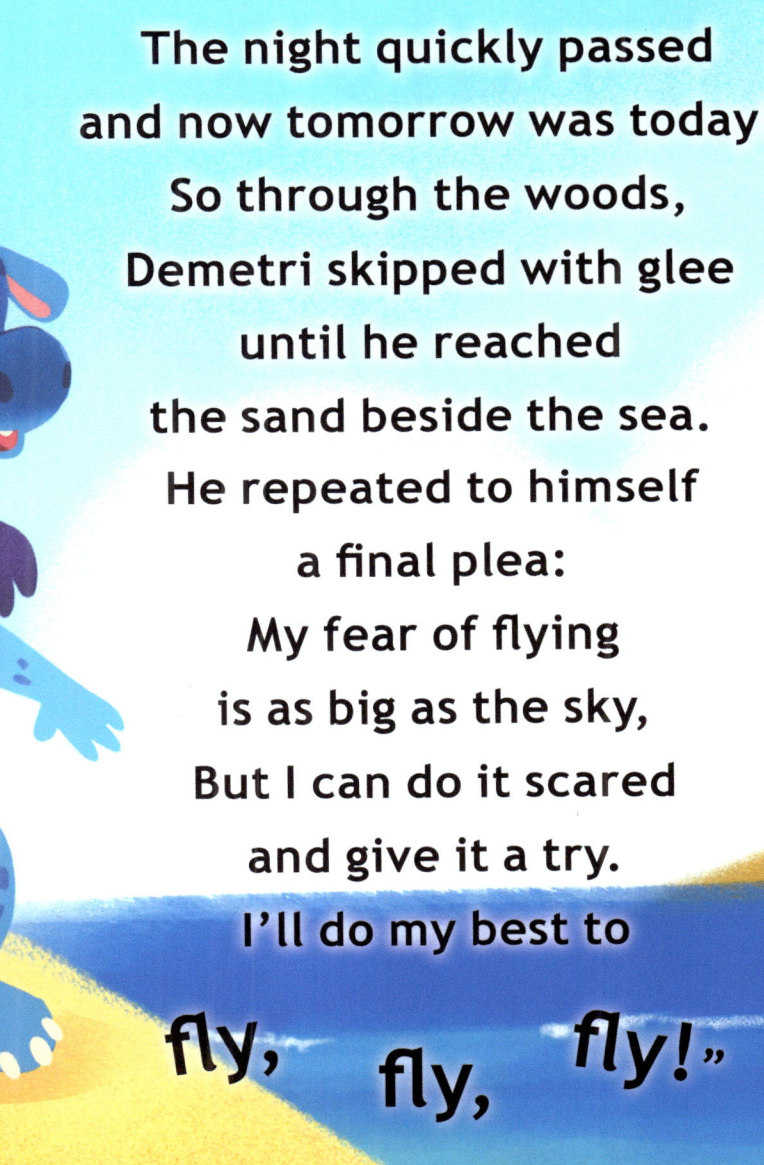

The night quickly passed
and now tomorrow was today!
So through the woods,
Demetri skipped with glee
until he reached
the sand beside the sea.
He repeated to himself
a final plea:
My fear of flying
is as big as the sky,
But I can do it scared
and give it a try.
I'll do my best to
fly, fly, fly!"

FLAP, FLAP, FLAP, JUMP!
One, two, three!

WOW!

Demetri lifted off the ground and was high above the sea!

Even his wings that were oh so small had no trouble holding Demetri who was oh so tall.

His little wings were stronger than he ever knew,
and now he was flying with an amazing view!

Back to his cave he flew and soared.
He flew all day long until he could no more.

Greeted by his mom, she was smiling ear to ear.
She gave him a hug and kiss, and began to cheer:

"You were brave today! I am so proud.
You didn't give up and now you're flying in the clouds!

You were scared to fly and that's okay.

You kept trying and did it scared—
that's what it means to be brave!"

Julie Ivers

Julie's joy for writing began long ago in 5th grade when she wrote a fun poem about how much she loved pizza. Now as a new mom, she enjoys writing playful and encouraging children's stories that teach important values about life. She graduated with a Bachelor of Arts degree from Brigham Young University—Idaho, and resides in American Fork, Utah, with her husband, Dustin, son, Trey, and daughter, Claire. Julie also loves crafting, baking, horseback riding, yoga, and spending time outside in the sun with family.

Diana Hernandez is a character artist and children's book illustrator with a visual design and animation background. She lives in sunny Nicaragua with her old friend, the corgi dog, Peggy. Her love for nature and fantasy creatures inspires her to create colorful and educational stories for kids and her inner child. You can follow her art at:
https://www.behance.net/ddianahernandez and Instagram @diana.illustr

Diana Hernandez

**Want more insightful, empowering, fun children's books?
Want activities and links to go along with the story?**
Visit us at lawleypublishing.com

For updates and info on New Releases follow us at

lawleypublishing   @kidsbookswithheart

Printed in the USA
CPSIA information can be obtained
at www.ICGtesting.com
LVHW070054020824
787105LV00006B/52